We're Going on a Picnic!

PAT HUTCHINS

We're Going on a Picnic!

RED FOX

ALSO BY PAT HUTCHINS

Rosie's Walk
The Shrinking Mouse
Don't Forget the Bacon
Ten Red Apples

WE'RE GOING ON A PICNIC!
A RED FOX BOOK 0 09 943304 4

Published in Great Britain by The Bodley Head,
an imprint of Random House Children's Books

The Bodley Head edition published 2002
Red Fox edition published 2003

First published by Greenwillow Books, New York 2002

1 3 5 7 9 10 8 6 4 2

Copyright © Pat Hutchins, 2002

The right of Pat Hutchins to be identified as the author and illustrator of this work
has been asserted in accordance with the Copyright, Designs and Patents Act 1988

Red Fox Books are published by Random House Children's Books,
61–63 Uxbridge Road, London W5 5SA,
a division of The Random House Group Ltd,
in Australia by Random House Australia (Pty) Ltd,
20 Alfred Street, Milsons Point, Sydney, NSW 2061, Australia,
in New Zealand by Random House New Zealand Ltd,
18 Poland Road, Glenfield, Auckland 10, New Zealand,
and in South Africa by Random House (Pty) Ltd,
Endulini, 5A Jubilee Road, Parktown 2193, South Africa

THE RANDOM HOUSE GROUP Limited Reg. No. 954009
www.kidsatrandomhouse.co.uk

A CIP catalogue record for this book is available from the British Library.

Printed in Hong Kong

FOR RACHEL ISA BAINES

"Let's go on a picnic,"
said Hen, Duck, and Goose.
"It's such a lovely day!"

So Hen picked some berries
(because Hen liked berries best),
and Goose picked some apples
(because Goose liked apples best),
and Duck picked some pears
(because Duck liked pears best).
And they put them in the basket.

"We're going on a picnic!" they sang
as they walked across the field.

"This looks like a nice place
for a picnic," said Hen,
and set the basket down.
"I can't wait to eat
some of those berries!"

"It's a bit shady," said Duck.
"Let's go up the hill.
 We might find an even nicer place."
"All right," said Hen,
"but it's your turn to carry the basket."

"We're going on a picnic!" they sang
as they walked up the hill.

"This looks like a nice place for a picnic,"
said Duck, and set the basket down.
"I can't wait to eat some of those pears!"

"It's a bit windy," said Goose.
"Let's go down the hill.
 We might find an even nicer place."
"All right," said Duck,
"but it's your turn to carry the basket."

"We're going on a picnic!" they sang
as they walked down the hill.

"This looks like a nice place for a picnic,"
said Goose, and set the basket down.
"I can't wait to eat some of those apples!"

"It's a bit hot," said Hen and Duck.
"Let's go down this path.
 We might find an even nicer place."
"All right," said Goose,
"but let's ALL carry the basket."

"We're going on a picnic!" they sang
as they walked around the lane.

"Oh!" they cried,
and set the basket down.
"We've walked back home,
and we haven't had our picnic!"

"Off we go again," said Hen.
But when they picked up the basket,
it was very light.

And very empty.

"Duck," said Hen, "did you eat the pears?"

"No," said Duck.

"Goose," said Hen, "did you eat the apples?"

"No," said Goose.

"Hen," said Duck and Goose, "did you eat the berries?"

"No," said Hen.

"Then they must have fallen out," said everyone
at the same time.

So Hen picked some more berries
(because Hen liked berries best),
and Goose picked some more apples
(because Goose liked apples best),
and Duck picked some more pears
(because Duck liked pears best).
And they put them in the basket.

"We're going on a picnic!" they sang
as they walked across the field.

"This looks like a nice place for a picnic,"
they all said, and set the basket down.